THE PERILS OF MONEY

ROBERT ROGERS

Gotham Books
30 N Gould St.
Ste. 20820, Sheridan, WY 82801
https://gothambooksinc.com/
Phone: 1 (307) 464-7800

Published by Gotham Books (July 14, 2022)

ISBN: 978-1-956349-94-8 (sc)
ISBN: 978-1-956349-95-5 (e)

CONTENTS

Acknowledgement

For my sister Nina
who provided excellent content suggestions

CHAPTER 1

A Lingering Vision

I FIND MYSELF IN LEAVENWORTH KANSAS in the bright summer sunlight or treading through the deep snow.

I've been here for the past five years since retiring as an Army officer five years ago in 1970. Leavenworth is a small town sitting close to the West bank of the Missouri River. It has a small population of thirty-seven thousand. It was founded in 1827 and is the first city incorporated in the territory of Kansas. In the years before the Civil war, Leavenworth was a hotbed of anti-slavery, often leading to open physical confrontations on the street and in public meetings. Unfortunately, it is best known for its prisons. A United States Penitentiary is located on Fort Leavenworth. Leavenworth is about 31 miles Northwest of Kansas City. Oddly enough Kansas City is in Missouri. While fighting as an Infantry officer in Vietnam I was a Captain advising South Vietnamese Infantry soldiers. I spent two tours there. While I was in Vietnam I was promoted to Major and after the second tour I was promoted to Lieutenant Colonel and assigned to Fort Leavenworth to teach Infantry tactics to officers' classes at the U.S. Army Command and General Staff College. It is the Center for Army Leadership and the School of Advanced Military Studies. I decided to buy a house in Leavenworth County. Lots of trees and grass.

I'm a rather solitary man. As a younger man I attended the University of California and received a master's degree. Fortunately, over the years I have had several girlfriends, but I never married. I sometimes wish I had married. I go up on Post each week to buy essential items in the PX and to the Commissary to purchase food items. I don't buy much food each visit since it just spoils before I get around to eating it. I rarely go to restaurants. I just cook at home. I have so many hobbies that I have trouble finding enough time deal-ing with them. I write fictional books and poem books, play the guitar, paint, restore antique cars, do carpenter work, collect, and listen to vinyl recordings among other things.

Yesterday I drove six miles to Bob's Grocery store to buy some MASA. It's not stocked in the Commissary. Bob's is the closest retail store. I really like fixing Mexican food. The store was busy. I had a difficult time finding a place to park my 1974 Chevy. It's a convert-ible. There was little wind, and the top was down. I could even wear my cowboy hat without it blowing off. I carefully walked toward the front door and watched for the multitude of cars that were hunting parking spaces. Two adjacent glass front doors could be pushed open. I entered the door that was identified with a sign that said ENTER. I began to search for MASA the preferred flower I like to make soft tortillas. I began to search through the aisles. I slowly searched moving my eyes from left to right in the search. I bumped into a young woman and we both were a bit startled. I began to apologize, and she smiled and asked if I was looking for something. I said yea I was looking for some MASA. She said maybe I can help. I said I would be grateful; I need some help. She was pushing a small cart with a few canned items in it. She pointed and said why don't we go this way over to the isle identified as baking items. Seemed logical. She released the cart and motioned me to follow her. I said do you want to take the cart with us? She waved her hand and said no I'll just leave it here and get it later. There was a brief jester for me to follow her. As she walked, I noticed she was wearing some black slacks that fit rather tight and a white blouse that loosely covered a rather full bust. I thought the combination was rather attractive, sexy. She looked back over her left shoulder just to make sure I was following. We walked through several aisles and searched. She stopped, pointed to a bottom shelf, and said I think we found some. I moved forward, bent down, and retrieved two bulky paper packages. I looked up and said I really thank you. I asked can you now find that cart you were pushing? I hope so. I said let me go with you. I feel a bit guilty for separating you from the items you had in the cart. She looked me straight in the eyes and said I seldom loose the thing I really want. She said my name is Layla. My name is Jacob, most just call me Jake. We both went to the checkout area. Waited for a register to be free. I let her buy the canned items first. After they gave her the receipt, I put the MASA packages on the counter. We both gathered our paper sacked items and walked to the exit. I opened the door. Once outside she paused and looked at me. She said would you like to walk over to McDonalds and get a cup of coffee? She pointed and said we could go over to that place on the corner, but I really don't like the coffee and it costs too much. I said I'll put my sack in the car and meet you at the McDonald's entrance. I watched her walk to her car. I guessed it was a 1969 or 1970 Ford Mustang. I was impressed. Many these days are driving a car with an automatic transmission. I didn't know if the car was hers, her dad's, or husband's. Curious. I met her just inside McDonalds. We both ordered coffee. I volunteered to pay. We found a table and sat down. I asked if she owned the Ford.

She said yes. Why would you own an antique Ford? She grinned and said I like them, I bought it a couple years ago from a guy that had a Ford collection and needed to get rid of some. It's fun to drive. I needed to refresh my ability to drive it, but it came naturally and now I have no trouble. I toasted her with my coffee cup and said I have a couple of antique VWs. She seemed impressed. She said do you collect them? I said I generally restore them and sell them but the best car I keep. I always elect to keep the best one. We quietly sat there and sipped our small cup of coffee. She raised her head, looked at me and asked are you married? I sipped a bit of coffee, looked directly at her, and said No, are you? She leaned back and said I once was but not now. I said Well that makes two of us. She said Leavenworth is a rather small town and asked if I lived here. I said Yes, I live out in the Leavenworth County in a house I bought while teaching soldiers at Fort Leavenworth. She asked are you a soldier? I said I use to be, but I quit active duty and just resorted to teaching. She asked what do you teach? I teach Infantry Tactics. She looked down at her coffee cup and said that's interesting. Since she asked me where I lived, I ask where she lived. She said I rent a house on 5th street. I nodded and said you live rather close, perhaps we could have dinner sometime. She said that would be nice. She said I seldom venture out for dinner I just cook something simple at home. I chuckled and said so do I and I'm getting to be a lot better cook. She said maybe you could teach me a few things.

Perhaps I can. Where do you work? She said I'm a Medical Doctor, made a jester with her left hand over her right shoulder and said I work over there at the Saint John's Hospital. I leaned over and took out my billfold and extracted what appears to be a business card, but it is simply a card that I had printed with my name, phone number, and address and I handed it to her, she looked at it and said I'll call you next week and you can come over and we can cook something we both like. I said OK. She asked if I had another card so she could write her phone number on the back of it. I handed her another card, she wrote the phone number and handed it back to me. We got up, walked out the door, and proceeded to our cars. I stopped and watched her open the door to that Ford. She cranked it up. It sounded great. She slowly pulled out from the parking space and headed north on 4th street. I saw her wave to me as she passed by the Chevy. What a nice old Ford, and what a nice woman. I smiled and said to myself I think she could teach me a few things. I carefully crawled in the seat, put my shades and cowboy hat on, started the car and carefully drove to the grocery store exit where it joined Eisenhower Road. I turned West. Eisenhower Road has two lanes and is badly pitted. A short but bumpy drive to the stop sign. I turned left to enter Tonganoxie Drive. Two and a half miles later I turned toward my house on a long gravel driveway. I stopped the car and walked to the post office box to retrieve the mail. There were two letters and three magazines, got back into the car, drove up to the garage door, got out of the car and opened the garage door. The garage door is rather heavy and needs a little muscle to lift it completely. The Chevy was still running, and I slowly pulled it into the garage. I got out of the car, unlocked the trunk with my trunk key, picked up the MASA package and enter the door to the small laundry room. When I got back to the house, I couldn't get her out of my mind. Her vision just seemed to linger.

She called me at 10:05 on Sunday and left a message to call her back. I had driven on Post to go to the PX and Commissary to pick up a few items and get some gas. The gas station is primarily a liquor store. It has all the beer and hard liquor brands and a large array of wines. The entrance to the Post has contract guards that check every entering car. They look at the military ID card and approve entering. They usually say to me "enjoy the day, Colonel." On rare occasions some nut attempts to enter the Post without stopping at the checkpoint. The car doesn't get very far because in a short distance from the guard post a wide metal plate that has large, pointed prongs attached can be automatically raised by the guards. When a car hits the prongs both front tires are punctured, and the car is held at that spot. When I returned to the house, I called her at about 1:00. She answered and said Hello this is Loyla do you remember me? I paused and then said sure I remember you I sure wouldn't forget. She said instead of us having dinner why don't we meet for lunch. I said sure it sounds good to me. She asked do you like barbeque. Who wouldn't like barbeque here in Kansas? Kansas City is renowned for its barbeque places and the unique barbeque preparation has spread to its adjacent areas including Leavenworth. I said sure. The first Kansas City notable barbeque was available in the 1920s. It was cooked outdoors in a pit, removed, and wrapped in newspaper. She suggested we meet the next Saturday, at a very small restaurant. She said it's close to your house and close to where I work, I'm sure it's open on Saturday but I think its closed on Sunday. That sounds good to me I'll meet you at the bar just inside the front door. There is no waiter to seat us so we can just pick any table. The name of the restaurant is Best

BBQ. It only serves BBQ. It is located at the junction of Eisenhower Road and 4th Street. For some strange reason the main north bound road headed toward Leavenworth starts at the new interstate highway called I-70 and changes designation four times before it terminates at Leavenworth: 73d Street, 7th Street, Main Street, 4th Street. It's the same road! She suggested we meet at 12:30.

On Saturday I drove to the BBQ place, found a place to park in the small restaurant parking area. Arrived at 12:15. There were about 15 parked cars. I went into the restaurant, sat on a barstool at the bar and ordered an Early Riser Boulevard beer and a glass. I don't' like to drink from a bottle. Layla walked in and with a finger taped me gently on my right shoulder. I turned, nice to see you, shall we find a table? Do you want to sit outside? She perched her lips and nodded her head yes. I picked up my glass and we moved outside and found a table. There were only four tables outside. She was wearing very little makeup, no lipstick, and she has short-cut black hair, wore dark blue slacks with what I call a Safari Shirt, olive green. She Is so slim I thought she might need to gain about five pounds. We both ordered a barbeque sandwich. She just drank a glass of water. We ate without much conversation. When we finished, she insisted on paying the tab and I insisted on paying the tip. When we left, she wasn't driving the Ford Mustang rather she had a 1970 2-door Pontiac.

CHAPTER 2

A Winner

Two weeks later I called her and asked if she was ready to cook a meal at her house. She said yes. Why don't you arrive at my house about 6:00 tomorrow? She gave me her address. I went to bed that night thinking about her and what we might cook. At 5:00 on Sunday I put on some slacks, white shirt, and dress shoes. I found her house, parked on the street, approached her front door, and knocked. She opened the door and said you found the place. I said yes it was rather easy. As I entered the small living room there was a young woman sitting in a reclining chair. She got up and Loyla introduced her as her younger sister Ava. We gently shook hands.

Layla said I know you like Mexican so why don't you show me the best, easiest way to make some spicy enchiladas, I think I have all the ingrediencies. She pointed to Ava and said I invited my younger sister to join us because she wants to meet you and she likes Mexican food. I smiled at Ava and said if you are interested, I recommend you watch us and you can easily learn how to make enchiladas. She laughed and said I plan to do that. Loyla and Ava looked so much alike they could be twins. They both set plates and silverware on the table and when the enchiladas were removed from the oven, we placed the large serving plate on some dishtowels that were spread on the table along with a salad Loyla made. I mixed an oil and vinegar dressing. We talked and one of the subjects related to the mail we often receive. Loyla said she continually received advertising documents she simply discarded but she often filled out the advertisements offering prize money. I said I do to. I leaned back in my chair and said the chance of winning one of those money prizes was extremely slim. They both shook their heads in agreement. We all quietly chuckled. I told them a story about what happed to my mailbox.

About two weeks earlier I walked up to get the mail and discovered my mailbox post was completely destroyed and the box was detached and laying on the grass, it was clear that some car had hit it. There was a lot of sheet metal and parts of a front headlight scattered in the area. I could tell from the parts that it must have been a relatively new car. I returned to the house, got my wheelbarrow out of the barn, took it up to the mailbox area and picked up all the car parts. I dumped the parts in front of my garage. I called the Police. The Police arrived in one car. I told them what I thought happened and showed them the car parts I dumped. One Policeman said he would place a Police car on Tonganoxie drive and wait to see if they could spot a car that had damage to the right side. He speculated that the driver might be someone traveling to and from work. I told him that the driver was probably drunk. I had to build a new wood post to hold the mailbox. Dad was a carpenter, I learned considerable carpenter skills, so I knew how to construct a solid, hefty post. Instead of using the old mailbox, I bought a bigger one at the hardware store and mounted it. Since I live out in the County and Leavenworth has limited retail facilities, I purchase a lot of things through the mail and the larger mailbox makes it easier for many items to be placed in the box rather than delivered to my front porch.

A month later I was up early and began my exercise routine. I pull on a pair of Levies, a sweatshirt, and some bathroom slippers and go down in the basement and do some bench presses, then I go upstairs back to the bedroom and take my clothes off. I run naked. Almost naked, I wear a sweatband around my forehead and put on a pair of sneakers. Then I head into a small bedroom that I have converted into an exercise room. I lie down, hook my toes under the end of a single sleeping bed that is still in the room and do sixty sit-ups. Then I turn on the TV and begin a two-mile run on a treadmill. The TV antenna is mounted on a metal pole on the backside of the house. I would prefer to run outside but out in the Country where I live there are no sidewalks and running on the road is a bit danger-ous. The first treadmill was actually used as a form of punishment to punish prisoners. My new treadmill was difficult getting down a narrow hall and through the exercise room door. When it was deliv-ered two men unloaded it. The three large parts were wrapped in a single box. I asked if they would put it into the house. They said no. So, I asked them to put it on the front porch where I could open the box and drag those three large pieces into the house. I exercise every morning. It's a habit that I started when entering the Army. When I don't exercise, I feel guilty. I even did some sit-ups and push-ups when I was in Vietnam. I didn't need to run since I was mostly in a combat situation and carrying a PRC-25 backpack radio that weighed twenty pounds. The maximum transmitting distance was about ten miles.

As I was running on Saturday morning, I heard a vehicle stop in front of my house. I thought it was probably a delivery truck delivering a package, so I didn't stop my run. Besides I was naked and didn't want to go to the door. Actually, it was Loyla in her Pontiac. She opened the house front door, and she could hear me running. She followed the noise down the hall to the open door of the exercise room. When she saw me, she put her hand lightly over her mouth and said OH I'm sorry. I said don't be, I didn't hear you come in. She said I need to talk to you. I looked at her and said I need to run another mile and take a shower. It won't take me long. Why don't you go into the kitchen and fix us a cup of coffee? The red coffee can is next to the stove.

Normally after my run I put some water in a bucket and with a sponge I wipe off the treadmill running belt. I sweat profusely and it drops on the belt. I feel compelled to wipe it down. Since Loyla is here I will wipe it down later.

As we drank the coffee, she said she had received a call from a publishing agency and told her she was the winner of a large amount of prize money, and they wanted to come out of Kansas City to her house along with a radio crew to record the reward presentation. She thought it might well be some kind of prank. I said when did they say they would arrive. They asked me for an appropriate time, and I skeptically said at about 1:00 next Saturday. I don't want them arriving later when its dark. I want someone to stand beside me and ensure that this is real.

She said you are a friend and a soldier, and would know what to do, I don't want to call the Police. No problem just let me know when I should be there.

She called me Friday morning and said they would arrive at the house at 1:00 in a van with two camera men to film the event. I said I'll be there.

I drove to Loyla's house and arrived at 12:30. She opened the door and when I stepped in Ava was standing there. Loyla said I appreciate you coming. I said hello to both her and Ava. We waited inside. At 1:18 the van parked on the curb. My Rolex keeps good time. Loyla and I stepped outside. The van had KLINE INVESTMENT painted on the side and had a Missouri license plate. A tall man approached and said he was Grant Thompson representing Kline Investment. He asked are you Loyla Carter? She nodded yes. He said I'm overjoyed to be here to present the award of 25.000 for the first month and 25,000 each month for the next five years. I need to tell you a lot more but first I need to verify that I am awarding this prize to the right person. Can you show me a government document with your picture indicating you are Loyla Carter? A driver's license or passport would be fine. Loyla nodded and said I need to go into the house and get my purse. He nodded and stood there with his hands clasped in front of him. He said nothing. Loyla returned and showed him a driver's license. He pointed at me and asked Loyla if I was her husband. She said no he is Colonel Anderson a friend. He said while the crew gathers their cameras, he would tell her what would happen next. I will explain what we will do here and then tell you how we will award you the money. I would like for you and me to stand together so we can use one microphone and let the crew record the presentation.

The actual money will be deposited in a bank you prefer. I will ask you to open a new bank account in your name and the Kline Investment agency will wire the money to that account. What bank do you do business with? She said I bank with American Forces Bank. They have two banks here; one is on Fort Leavenworth and the other is on 4th Street across from the drug store. I can't enter Fort Leavenworth, so I use the bank on 4th Street. He said I will be the presenter, but I am also a Lawyer for Kline Investment. If you have the time today, I will accompany you to the bank and help you establish an account and let the bank know that we will be depositing money to the account. The first twenty-five thousand will be deposited in about three days.

The presentation broadcast will be aired by several radio stations including Kansas City. When the money is transferred, I will come back, meet you to sign a receipt for the money.

The radio presentation was made, and the van followed Loyla and me over to the bank. Grant and Loyla entered the bank and created the account. When we left the bank, I asked why Ava didn't come outside. She said she just didn't want to be part of the presentation. When we got back to the house, I said why don't the three of us go over to Weston, spend the remainder of the afternoon, and have dinner. Both looked a bit surprised, and Ava said I don't think either of us have ever been to Weston. Weston is a small town just a bit smaller than Leavenworth. It's the oldest town in Missouri. It's across the bridge about nine miles on the East side of the Missouri river. I said the main street in Weston has about three restaurants that have excellent food and Main Street only has interesting antique stores. I looked at Loyla and said you may want to spend some of that twenty-five thousand you just received. We all laughed. If we go, I said we will have to take your Ford, your Pontiac and my Chevy only have two seats. Loyla pushed a finger into my stomach and said since you know how to get there, you drive.

CHAPTER 3

Sexual Questions

L OYLA AND I MET SEVERAL times over the next three months and shared our likes, dislikes, and future aspirations. We were truthful and enjoyed each other's company. We kissed each time we met. On one occasion she was in my house, and we drink a couple glasses of wine. I had been practicing my guitar playing. I'm a complete novice. I have written several songs and assigned some of the cords to the songs. I have learned how to finger the six Major Open cords and the four minor cords. The term Major Open cords have that name because there is always an open string when all the strings are strummed. As we sat on the couch watching the TV program, I said since you are a doctor, would you be offended if I asked you some questions I have about men and women sexual experiences? She looked at me and said fill this glass again and ask whatever you want. I filled both glasses and turned the TV volume down. I said I have always been puzzled as to what sexual activity best satisfies a man and a woman. I obviously know something about men but not women. She looked attentive and said yes tell me what you want to know. Well as I understand, primarily women have different desires. A man typically just tries to have sex fast and reach orgasm. I don't think that is very satisfying for a woman. She looked at me and said no it isn't. I said my brief research indicates that women even when married masturbate about twice each month, some even more. Is that right? Yes, it is. I asked is that a healthy practice. She said masturbation for both men and women is a natural experience and can even result in relieving stress. It can have a calming effect and it is not unhealthy or dangerous. I said men seem to masturbate more often. She had no reply. I said would it be alright if I asked more specific, detailed questions. I would really like to understand what excites a woman. She chuckled and said go ahead. I shifted in my seat and moved to an adjacent recliner leaned toward her and began to ask specific questions. Men seem to university think the longer their penis the better they can satisfy a woman, but it seems that length is not that important. The grith seems to be as important. Loyla said that is essentially correct. There is no penis too large. Remember the vagina can open enough to birth a baby. OK, let me ask another question. Take another sip of that wine and I will ask. She sipped a drink set the glass down on the coffee table and then I said the clitoris seems to be the most sexually sensitive area. How in the world can a man during sex excite that area? She thought for a moment and said it is rather difficult. A man on top with a grinding motion rather that pumping action seems to be the best method. Also remember that women can experience multiple climaxes. Men typically stop and withdraw after climax. I nodded and said that is true. Are lubricates needed? She said they can be used and helpful, but saliva is the best. I know that seems unsanitary, but it is the best lubricant. Just soft licks. It can be applied to the penis or vulva. You just must find a willing partner. She said all women are different, it is best to ask her what she likes. I said does a woman like her body stroked. OH yes, stroking anywhere on the body can be exciting. I asked, the breasts. Well yes but other parts are also turn-ones. She held both palms up and said as you well know stroking the body of a man can also be pleasurable for him. Few women seem to know how well that can please a man. I agreed. One last strange question. Why do women shave their pubic area? Is it for sanitary reasons? It seems a little dangerous to me. Loyla dipped her head and said not all women do that, but the primary reasons seem to be they feel more feminine, younger. It may not be the best decision because each hair is attached to a nerve and that can increase greater sexual satisfaction. I don't. She looked at me and calmly said would you like to experiment? I stood, took her hand, and lead her to the back bedroom. We essentially undressed each other and claimed on top of the bed. I followed her sexual advice. When we stopped, we were both exhausted. The bed covers were a bit wrinkled. After a bit she turned, looked at me, smiled and said you have learned a lot. I said yea it's like playing my guitar I just need more practice. We laughed. After a time we got off the bed and showered together. The hot water felt good, we toweled off, dressed, and went back into the living room. I said relax, listen to the recording of Patsy Cline and a new record by Bobbie Gentry and I will fix some pasta. We talked from the kitchen to the living room, and she loudly said I noticed you don't have any tattoos, they seem to be coming popular for Sailors and Soldiers. I said I hate needles and I think those that decide to have tattoos are a bit silly. I've lost enough blood. I asked do you think they are attractive. She leaned forward, placed both balm of her hands on her knees and loudly said NO.

CHAPTER 4

Popularity Problem

W HEN LOYLA RETURNED TO WORK at the hospital her asso-
ciates congratulated her and asked a lot of questions con-
cerning winning the prize. She was also inodiated with
phone calls including the local television and radio stations that
wanted comments. The KC radio station asked if they could come to
Leavenworth and interview her. She didn't want that popularity. Ava
was also receiving phone calls. One or two callers asked when Loyla
would receive the money and in what bank did she plan to deposit
the money. Ava wondered how people found her phone number and
why would they call her and ask personal questions. Those phone
calls seemed a bit suspicious to me. I wonder why anyone would ask
questions about a specific bank. I don't think they are interested in
robbing the bank for Loyla' 25,000. The bank has plenty of money.
Either the caller is just inquisitive or has some strange reason for
calling Ava and asking a question about a bank deposit that is wired
directly to the bank by Kline Investment.

I called the Saint John's hospital, got the receptionist, and asked to talk to Doctor Loyla. The receptionist said she is not currently available. I said please tell her that Jacob called and wants to talk to her. The receptionist asked if I was a patient. I said no but I need to talk to her. In about an hour Loyla called me back. I said I need to go to the Post Office and mail a couple of packages, are you free to meet me at the coffee shop next to the Post Office? She said Well I have some patient appointments but I'm free from twelve to one today, I'll meet you at the coffee shop. The coffee shop is a small restaurant that has great coffee and serves breakfast and lunch only. It has a note on the door that says, "In heavy winds do not open the door wide it comes off the hinges." I drove down and parked directly in front of the Post Office. I waited inside the coffee shop.

Loyla arrived ten minutes later and parked directly in front of my Chevy. We were seated and because it was lunch time, we both ordered soup, and coffee. She looked a bit perplexed and said Ava had called her and said she had noticed a black Buick Station Wagon parked in front of her house and it arrived every morning and no one got out. She even saw a guy with binoculars looking at her house. I said Well Ava is attractive and maybe some admirer has some fascination for her. She said yea maybe so but when Ava drives to work at the bank the car follows her and that upsets her. Ava is a cashier in the Armed Forces Bank on 4th street where Loyla banks. I asked does the Station Wagon follow her to other places. Loyla said yes, I think she told me that it did. I said why don't I go over to Ava's house on Sunday when she is not working and put her in my car, and we can see if the Buick follows us. You think Ava would go along with that. She said I don't know I will ask her and let you know. We finished eating, Loyla drove back to the hospital. I mailed my packages and drove home. I thought about calling the Police but there was no credible evidence that something was criminally wrong. Loyla called me that evening and said Ava would like for you to pick her up at about ten o'clock on Sunday. I said OK I'll be there.

I arrived at her house on time and Ava stepped out the front door, greeted me and said I'm glad you came. She pointed and said see that black Station Wagon that's the one that has two guys and keeps watching the house and following me to work. I looked but couldn't see anybody in the car. I said get in my car and we will drive around and see if we are followed. I opened the right-side car door so she could get in. I looked at her and said OK I'm going to drive around and see if the car follows us. I turned on 5th Street, headed to 4th Street, turned West on Summit and then turned right, on Broadway past the Goodwill store, turned East on Delaware, a one-way street. I kept looking in my rearview mirror and sure enough the Buick kept following us. I asked do you have you driver's license with you? She searched her purse and said yes here it is. I said good I'm going to head for the Post entrance. I can easily get me and you through the entrance gate and we shall see if the car can follow us. In three minutes, we arrived at the gate, and I showed the guard my ID card and Ava's driver's license. As I paused at the gate, I told the guard that the black Buick two cars behind me was constantly following us all through town for no reason. I said I don't think they have legal access to the Post and it might be wise to check them out. The guard said no problem I'll be sure and see if they have a right to enter the Post at this gate, if not I will tell them to go to the visitor entrance gate. I said they may crash through this gate just to follow us. He said if they do that, I can easily stop them with the barrier plate.

I quickly headed toward the Commissary entrance. As I turned left, I could see the Buick didn't stop at the entrance and was speeding to catch-up to us. The guard immediately actived the barrier. The second guard at the second entrance gate signaled for all the waiting cars to stop.

The Buick crashed into the pronged barrier and was impaled there. The Buick doors on the right and left side opened and two men leaped out and began running back toward the right side of the Post entrance. One guard ran to the impaled car. An MP car with all the lights on headed toward the entrance but the MP car couldn't cross the barrier because it was still up. The two MPs and the gate guard began to investigate the impaled car. I drove into the gas station parked and waited. Twenty minutes later an MP car pulled up, parked, and two MPs got out and walked to my car. I got out. They asked a lot of questions and asked if we could identify the two guys who ran. I said no I wish we had, and finally they said Colonel thanks for your information the Station Wagon has been removed and cars can now enter and leave the Post. We will let the Leavenworth Police know what happened and ask them to see if they can identify who owns that Buick and locate the two men that escaped. How can we get in touch with you? I gave them a card. We have a license plate number. I thanked them and I got into the car with Ava and headed back to her house. She looked upset but didn't say much. I said why don't you call Loyla or go over to the hospital and tell her what hap-pened. When we got to her house, she immediately called the hospital, identified herself as Loyla's sister and asked the receptionist to tell Loyla to call her. About thirty minutes later Loyla returned the call. Ava told her what had happened and then handed the phone to me and said Loyla wants to talk to you. Loyla asked "What's going on?" I said I didn't know but it seems serious. I said why don't you and Ava come over to my house for a couple of days just to be sure things quiet down and no one can easily find you or Ava. I have three bedrooms and plenty to eat and a large variety of wines. There was a long pause and she finally said OK give the phone back to Ava. Ava cupped her hand around the phone and spoke softly so I couldn't hear their conversation. Ava put the phone in the cradle and said OK let's go over to your house and my sister will join us at about six o'clock. At 6:15 a Pontiac arrived and parked in front of my house and Loyla got out and opened the front door. She and Ava hugged. I said why don't you both take a look at the wine rack and pick something you like. I will place them in the refrigerator just to chill them. They began to search through the wine rack that I had placed on a table. I said I have three bedrooms, there are two bathrooms so just pick a bedroom you want to sleep in, I'll take the third one. All of them are made-up and I have the air conditioning turned up so they all should be cool. You can also turn on a fan that is in the room. I suspect you didn't bring a change of clothes, so you are stuck with the clothes you have on. If you need to wash anything, just put the items in the washer tonight and you can wash and dry them. I won't watch. I'll get them out in the morning and hand them to you just as you slightly open your bedroom door. All three of us listened to some of the records I have collected. Lots of country songs. At 11:30 and after three glasses of wine Ava said I need to get some sleep if I can. I said OK as she got up and headed for the back bedroom. I quietly said to Loyla I would prefer if you crawled into bed with me, but I don't think your sister would approve. She looked at me and said that's a good idea, but I agree, maybe in a few days when this whole thing is solved.

They didn't place anything in the washer. I fixed some breakfast with some alvocado slices, toast, and boiled eggs, and accompanied it with some canalope slices, tomato chunks with a choice of orange juice and coffee. They seemed to like the selections. I walked up the driveway at 9:32 and picked-up the newspaper and walked back to the house. As I stepped inside the door Loyla said I need to go into town. I said why? She said Ava needs some Tampons. She didn't bring any with her. I said why don't you take my car rather than yours just as a precaution.

Your Pontiac might be recognized. I took the keys off the keyboard where it hangs keys. I said the shifting pattern is a bit different, but you should have no problem finding the right gears. I think you will find what you need in Bob's Grocery. It's close.

Loyla returned in about forty-five minutes. She got out of the car holding a small paper package. When she come into the house, she handed me the car keys and handed Ava the package. Ava said nothing but walked down the hall to her bedroom.

CHAPTER 5

A Search

THE NEXT MORNING, I CALLED the Leavenworth Police, identified myself and asked if they had a record of finding the owner of the Buick Station Wagon or the two men that fled. Some Police official got on the line and said the Station Wagon had been stolen and the license plate identified the owner as an elderly man living in Kansas City. That Buick was stolen about two weeks ago. The Kansas City Police Department reported it had been stolen. I hoped that maybe the problem has come to an end.

I told Loyla and Ava about the stolen vehicle and suggested that they could probably return to their homes. Loyla said yes, I need to get back to the house and do some clothes washing and get back to work. Ava nodded her head and said so do I. I said OK if anything strange or suspicious happens just give me a call. If you feel real danger, call the Police. Loyla turned to face me and asked will you be returning on Post to teach? I said no I check-in every day usually by phone.

The student soldiers have been here for about a year and completed their training. Most will soon be reassigned and there won't be a second group assigned here for a couple of months. When the new group arrives, I will be teaching. In the meantime, I am essentially free. I do plan to go on Post later today to get some dish washing soap, some razor blades, and another pair of reading glasses. My real reason was to talk to the gate guard that had stopped that Station Wagon. I drove up to the gate guard, he was the one I wanted to talk to. I showed him my ID and then drove through the gate a short distance and parked on the far-right side of the gate. I got out of the car and went back to talk to the guard. There were no cars waiting to enter the Post. I said I'm one of the individuals involved in the stopping of that Station Wagon. He said yaw I recognized your Chevrolet. I asked what happened to that Station Wagon. He said we didn't have much trouble getting it off the barrier and the Leavenworth Police had it towed away. I asked was their anything in it that would help identify who those two men were. He said no the Police said the car seemed to be completely clean except for two handguns the Police found.

There was a .45 automatic and a .22 revolver. I said I hope the serial numbers on the guns will help lead them to those two guys. He grinned and said I don't think so. The guns were probably stollen. The gun stores don't even record the serial numbers when they are sold. Maybe someday that will change. When Jim and I were talking to the Police they asked if either of us could identify those two guys. I said sure Jim and I both got a good look when they got out of the car and started running away. The cops asked if Jim and me would come down to the Police station and describe them. They would have a sketch artist prepare some pictures based on our descriptions. He said they would prepare some wanted posters and distribute them in public places in Leavenworth and Kansas City. I said thanks for the information, I see a car coming that wants to enter. I walked back to the Chevy, put the key in the ignition, cranked the starter and drove down to the PX. Since I'm on Post I might as well buy those razer blades and go over to the gas station and get some Club Soda for that Bourbon I have sitting next to that wine rack.

When I got back to the house, I called Loyla at the hospital. I said I don't want to take much of your time because I know you are busy, but I have some information I want to tell you. In addition, I need a little more advice and practice. She said why don't you come over tomorrow evening at about seven. Every time we meet, we seem to go somewhere to eat or fix dinner. Why don't I fix something this time? I said you want me to bring anything. Yes, bring that bottle of Sangria you have in that wine rack. By the way I won't ask Ava to join us. I said I'll see you at seven tomorrow.

I took out that bottle of Sangria and put it in the fridge. I thought about that sexual advice she gave me and thought I would ask her what she would like me to do. Medical Doctors don't seem to get embarrassed or reluctant to give advice. I've learned some new things.

I got to her house at 5:45. She met me at the front door. I held the wine out and said where would you like me to sit this. She pointed to the dining room table and said I'll find the corkscrew.

Come into the kitchen and tell me what you know. I asked if she was ready for some wine. She said OK but you can only drink one glass so you may want to wait and have it with these pork chops and mashed potatoes. I asked why only one glass. She turned from the stove with a wood spatula in her hand, pointed it at me and said because too much alcohol reduces your ability to perform well. OH, is said, more good advice. I said I brought some Viagra should I take it. She chuckled. You can if you want but take it right after dinner. It won't be effective for about an hour. I said yea my Army doctor told me that when he wrote the prescription.

As we ate, I told her about the conversation with the gate guard and said I hope those Police posters help find those two guys.

I got up from the table and took a glass out of an upper cabinet filled it with water and swallowed the Viagra capsule I had in my shirt pocket. She looked at me and smiled. We moved into the Living Room, turned on the TV and watched a Combat episode starring Vick Morrow and Laramie Jason. The episode took one hour. We turned and looked at one another and silently got out of our chairs, Loyla turned off the television. She took my hand and we walked to her bedroom. An hour and a half later we put our clothes on and returned to the kitchen to wash and dry the dishes. She washed and I dried. As she put the dishes in the cabinet she said you have learned a lot about women, at least one woman and I have learned a lot about men, at least one man. We drank the rest of the wine.

Five days later I got a call from a Police Captain who said his Chief Officer asked him to call me and tell me that a citizen had probably recognized the two felons from a poster in a KC Driver License Office. I asked do you know were to find them. He said we are searching.

Loyla called me and said she had been trying to contact Ava for the past two days. She said she went over to Ava's house; the front door was not locked but Ava wasn't in the house. She said this is unusual we always talk to each other every day. I said I am going over to the Police station and tell them that Ava is missing. The Chief of Police said the KC Police department has located the fugitives' rented apartment and they have dispatched two vehicles. When the Police found the apartment, they knocked on the door and announced they were the KC Police and shouted open the door. They received no reply. One of the officers kicked the door open and three Police officers began to search the apartment. They found Ava with her hands behind her and tied to a bed railing. She was sitting down. When she saw the Police, she began to cry. The Police cut the ties. They were shoelaces tied together. Since the laces were narrow cords, they cut into her wrists. They asked her what had happened. She said three men had broken into her house at night through the back door, put her in a car and took her to this KC house. They didn't ask her any questions they just tied her to the bed and then left the apartment. The Police asked if they had hurt her in any way. She said no. She held out her arms and said my wrists hurt. She said three men looked at her laughed and made some rude remarks, but they didn't do anything to her but tie her to the bed. She said she needed a glass of water. A Policeman helped her stand up.

The Police said they would stake-out the apartment with an unmarked car and wait to see if the three men returned.

When Loyla got to her house she had a message shoved under her door that said we want you to give us fifty thousand dollars in one-hundred-dollar bills. If you don't you won't like what happens to your sister. Get the money from the bank tomorrow, put it in a box and deliver it tomorrow evening at seven. A red Ford will be waiting as you drive into the Cub Cadet mower dealer five miles south on

7th road. If you call the Police, we will know that, and you will not like what happens to your sister.

Loyla told me about the phone call. I said Ava has been found and the callers don't know that. I will go over to the Leavenworth Police and let them know what is happening. The Police told the Cub Cadet people what was happening and they would be in plain clothes and at the mower location long before seven o'clock. Loyla drove her Pontiac to the mower dealer location and waited inside her car. She carried a small, sealed box with newspapers in it. At about seven twenty a red Ford arrived, and a man got out and walked over to Loyla's car and said give me the box. Loyla reached over to the right seat, picked up the box and handed it to him through the car window. He began to walk back to the Ford. Four policemen drew their guns and arrested the two men in the Ford. The two were placed in a Police car and taken to the Leavenworth Police station. They were interrogated and asked where they could find their third companion. They initially refused. The Police told them that they would be charged with four felonies, car theft, avoiding arrest, attempted robbery and kidnapping that would probably result in a prison sentence of 20 to 25 years in prison but if you tell us who the third man is and how we can find him some of the lesser charges might be dropped. One of the guys hesitated then said I didn't know where he is, but he might be found in the bar on 81st street in Kansas City. What' his name? He goes by the name Jester. The KC Police found him two days later. The KC Police drove Ava back to Leavenworth when she was freed. It was late evening and she asked to go to Loyla's house. Loyla hugged her and said I know what happened, the Police told me. Let me see those wrist bruises, sit down and I will find my medical bag and get some gauze to wrap some ice on both wrists, they will feel cold but it's a good way to reduce the swelling and reduce the pain.

I wrote a letter thinking the Police for their work and sent a copy to the Leavenworth and Kansas City Police department.

CHAPTER 6

A Trip

OUR LIVES SETTLED DOWN AND we seemed to return to our normal routines. Winter was coming on and it was already getting a little chilly. I thought I probably should check my propane tank just to make sure I would have enough to warm the house. When I checked, the tank was down to a low 20%. I called Ferrellgas and requested that the tank be filled. It only provides fuel for the furnace. All the other appliances use electricity.

Loyla, Ava and I met often, talked, listened to my records, and drank the wine. On one occasion I said why don't the three of us get out of this small town and go somewhere where it is still warm. Ava said where would that be. I said maybe South into Florida or West to California. I pointed at Ava and said I'm sure your sister wouldn't object to paying for the trip. Loyla laughed and said I would gladly do that, but Ava and I have jobs here. I said Well yes but why don't you both simply take a vacation. I don't need to be back here for a couple of months. They both smiled and said they would consider my suggestion.

That next week when we were eating crackers and drinking a bit of wine at my house Ava said both of us think a vacation is a good idea. Where should we travel? I said how about California. I went to school there and know southern California rather well. Dad and I built a house there when I was a kid, and I would like to see if it is still standing. Rather than fly out there we might take the train. We can go directly from Kansas City to Santa Barbara. A train trip might be interesting. They both nodded. Loyla asked when should we go. I said that is entirely up to you and Ava, whenever you both can arrange for vacation time.

In early October Loyla had a friend that drove us to the Amtrak train station. The train rolled out for Santa Barbara. It's a straight trip without any station stops but it took two days to get there. The sleeping arrangements were OK, and the ride was pleasant.

When we got there, I rented a '73 4-door Plymouth. It wasn't popular but it was easy to drive. California had a lot of car traffic. Much more than I remember. We rented two rooms in the Seaside Hotel near the beach. Loyla and I occupied a single room. Ava didn't seem surprised or object. The next morning, we all met in the lobby and had some coffee. It was about 11:00 when we left the hotel and walked on the beach sand. Ava took her shoes of and walked barefooted.

She said this feels great, I've never walked on the ocean beach before. We got back to the hotel at about 2:30. I said how about we find a good restaurant and get some fresh fish. Leavenworth doesn't have any. They both looked down and Loyla said sounds like a good idea. I asked the hotel clerk if she could recommend a good fish restaurant in the near area. She said the Lure Fish House has excellent food and it is not far from here. I said can we walk to the restaurant. She said yes but I recommend you drive; I will draw you a road map to make sure you know how to get there, it's about half a mile away and only has one road turn from here.

We drove to the restaurant, parked, went inside, and enjoyed great food.

Our hotel room was on the third floor. A family with three kids were on the south side and made a lot of noise that we could hear in our room. That lasted until well after dark. On the other side a middle-aged man and wife turned their radio way up and we could easily hear it. The next day to escape all the distraction, we went outside and sat in the hotel's veranda, it was open on all four sides, but it had an overhead cover and six chairs. The chairs were wooden but had back and bottom cushioned pads that could be removed. We sat out there and enjoyed hearing the ocean waves and the cool breeze. I smoked a cigar that I had packed in a suitcase.

In the early evening while we were sitting in the veranda a tall man wearing a nice suite approached us and said Hello, you folks here on a vacation? I said yes, we are here from Kansas for a short period. He said I'm Charles Hagen and I live here and work for a real estate firm Estate Planners that has nationwide representatives. He asked where are you from in Kansas? I said a small town called Leavenworth, It's about 30 miles North of Kansas City. He said that's interesting we have an office in Kansas City. The Kansas City area seems to be growing rapidly. We are selling a lot of houses. Are you interested in buying a house? Loyla looked at me and said I'm not because I want to stay with my medical job, but my sister might be interested.

Overhearing our conversation, he looked at Loyla and said would you mind if I call one of our representatives in Kansas and see what is immediately available. Loyla said sure go ahead. He handed Loyla a business card and said he would call us at the hotel tomorrow morning after he had a chance to call his Kansas representative. When I call this hotel who should I ask for? I said call me and ask for Jacob. He nodded and said I'll do that. What time should I call? I said any time tomorrow morning.

I got the call the next morning at 10:46. Charles said I have talked to Betty our real estate representative in Kansas, and she says the firm has located three nice 3-bedroom homes for sale. I'm told the homes are in Olathe in a well-kept area and the homes are all in beautiful condition. He said I would like to give you pictures but it would take about five days for the pictures to arrive in the mail. I will contact Betty and have her call you and provide you the details about each house. I can give you her phone number, but you won't need it. About what time should I have her call? I said any time after 2:00 o'clock this afternoon.

When Ava joined us for coffee in the hotel reception room Loyla told her about the house offers and asked if she would be interested in buying a house. Ava hesitated and said Well I can think about it. I was with Loyla when the hotel clerk transferred Betty's call to Loyla's room. Betty described the three houses, and the Olathe landscape where the houses were located. She provided the house addresses for each house. Loyla wrote down the addresses and asked for the selling price. Betty said each house has a different selling price but the house she would recommend would cost 65,000 but only a 20,000 deposit would be needed.

That evening Charles showed up at the veranda and came over to talk to us. He asked if we had a chance to talk to Betty. I said yes. He said you need to decide rather quickly because the houses would probably be sold in the next few days. I asked how do we make a deposit payment. He said my company will provide you with a bank account number where you can wire the deposit. Loyla said yes, I know how that works. Charles said please thank about making the deposit by tomorrow.

When Charles left, I said to Loyla something seems a bit fishy. All this urgency seems strange. Why don't I call Baylor a buddy of mine in Leavenworth and ask him to go look at the houses? I can give him the addresses you wrote down.

I made the call to my buddy Baylor and asked if he could drive down to Olathe and look at the area and houses and let me know what he thinks about what he finds. He said sure I can go down there tomorrow morning, look at the houses and call you back late tomorrow evening. I said thanks I will be waiting for your call. The hotel number here is 886-4586, just ask for me.

Loyla and I stayed in our room beginning at 6:00 o'clock in the evening waiting for Baylor's call. He called at 9:00 and said I have some bad news. The addresses you gave me don't exist and there is no Estate Planners name listed in the White or Yellow Pages. I found the Local Post Officer and asked if they could identify the three addresses. They said no and they didn't know of any firm called Estate Planners. Either you gave me the wrong information, or someone is trying to steal your deposit money. I thought something was fishy.

When Charles met me in the hotel lounge the next morning I stood up from my chair, and when he got within my reaching range I grabber his string tie and pushed the knot hard against his throat.

He began to choke and couldn't talk. He grabbed my hands close to his neck and tried to pull them away from his tie. I said you stealing bastard I ought to strangle you. When he dropped to his knees on the hardwood floor, I hit him hard on the left side of his jaw. He fell sideways and couldn't get up. The hotel desk clerk ran over and said what's happening. I calmly said it's OK just me and a friend of mine having a disagreement. The clerk loosened the tie around Charles neck and helped him to his feet. Charles, if that is his real name, struggled to the front door and headed for his car. He could barley open the door and get in, but he did manage to get the key into the ignition, start the car, and drive out of the parking lot. I don't think we will see him again.

I got a cup of coffee, sat down, and slowly drank the coffee. Loyla came down looking for me. I said why don't you get Ava and I'll tell you what Baylor found. When we were all together, I repeated what Baylor told me and said I'm glad no money was wired from your bank account.

Ava asked if I had talked to Charles this morning. I said yea he and I had a slight disagreement and he left. I don't think he will contact any of us again.

CHAPTER 7

The Return

TWO DAYS LATER WE DROVE back to the train station, and I returned the rental car. In two days, we arrived back in Kansas City. I had asked Baylor to pick us up at the train station and drive us back to Leavenworth. Loyla and Ava still had vacation days, so I borrowed a 4-door car from a friend. For the next three weeks we enjoyed going back to Weston for the food and antiques and to the many KC museums. Once, we went to the small antique car museum where Loyla and I enjoyed looking at the cars and trying to name the old car makes.

As Loyla and I sat in her living room sipping Chardonnay she said having this money is a pain and causes me to want to give it away. I have a good job that I like, this house and my car are paid for, and I make enough money to live comfortably. I've been thinking about it and I've decided to give Ava enough money to buy a house here in Leavenworth and give the rest of the money to some of my patients and the remainder to three local charities. She looked at me and said if you want some just let me know how much you need. I smiled, paused, and said I don't need the money. I have saved over the years and put money in an investment firm that is doing well. I appreciate the offer, but I don't need it. I asked do you want us to continue seeing each other. She said yes, I would really like to be with you for a long time. There was a long pause and she said I was married once; I don't want to marry again. I smiled and said marriage is not always the wisest way to go. Let's just enjoy each other and practice what we already know.